STAR WARS®

THE CLONE WARS™

R2 TO THE RESCUE

adapted by Rob Valois

Grosset & Dunlap
An Imprint of Penguin Group (USA) Inc.
LucasBooks

GROSSET & DUNLAP

Published by the Penguin Group

Penguin Group (USA) Inc., 375 Hudson Street, New York, New York 10014, USA

Penguin Group (Canada), 90 Eglinton Avenue East, Suite 700, Toronto, Ontario M4P 2Y3, Canada

(a division of Pearson Penguin Canada Inc.)

Penguin Books Ltd., 80 Strand, London WC2R 0RL, England

Penguin Group Ireland, 25 St. Stephen's Green, Dublin 2, Ireland

(a division of Penguin Books Ltd.)

Penguin Group (Australia), 250 Camberwell Road, Camberwell, Victoria 3124, Australia

(a division of Pearson Australia Group Pty. Ltd.)

Penguin Books India Pvt. Ltd., 11 Community Centre, Panchsheel Park, New Delhi—110 017, India

Penguin Group (NZ), 67 Apollo Drive, Rosedale, North Shore 0632, New Zealand

(a division of Pearson New Zealand Ltd.)

Penguin Books (South Africa) (Pty.) Ltd., 24 Sturdee Avenue,

Rosebank, Johannesburg 2196, South Africa

Penguin Books Ltd., Registered Offices:

80 Strand, London WC2R 0RL, England

This book is published in partnership with LucasBooks, a division of Lucasfilm Ltd.

ISBN 978-0-448-45579-2   10 9 8 7 6 5 4 3 2 1

R2-D2 and his friend C-3PO were on their way home from the store. They were sent by their Master, Jedi Knight Anakin Skywalker, to pick up some last-minute supplies for a dinner party.

They needed to be careful because the city could be dangerous for two droids on their own. Anakin had told them to go straight to the store and then come right back home. He also warned them not to get lost or distracted.

Just then a strange little droid floated over to them. But the droids didn't listen to Anakin's warnings. R2-D2 got distracted and rolled off, leaving C-3PO alone with the droid.

"Artoo, where are you going?" C-3PO called out to his friend. But it was too late. The strange robot pushed him, and he tumbled backward into a waiting landspeeder. Before C-3PO realized what was happening, the speeder took off, leaving R2-D2 behind.

Trapped in the speeder, C-3PO couldn't see where the droid driver was taking him. Eventually they came to a stop and C-3PO was knocked from the speeder. Standing in front of him was the evil bounty hunter Cad Bane.

C-3PO looked at the blue-faced villain.
"Pardon me, sir," he said. "I believe there's been a terrible mistake."
"I don't think so," Cad Bane replied.

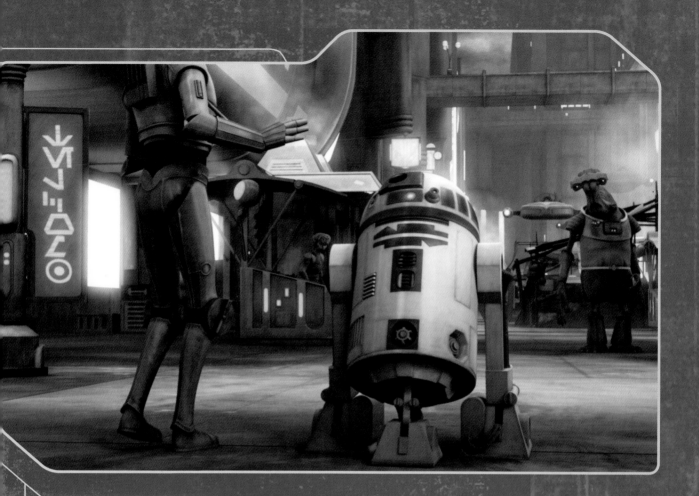

R2-D2 whistled as he rolled down the street. Suddenly he realized that C-3PO was no longer following behind him. He engaged his sensors and scanned the area. No luck. His friend was gone.

R2-D2 was worried and wondered if something terrible had happened to C-3PO. C-3PO was one of R2's oldest and closest friends, and R2 had learned that friendship is one of the most important things in the whole galaxy.

R2-D2 remembered one time when he was captured by the villainous General Grievous. R2 was all alone and was really scared.

General Grievous was looking for Republic secrets that R2-D2 had in his computer memory. R2 wouldn't tell Grievous anything, so the bad guys took R2-D2 apart to try to find where he'd hidden his secrets.

But R2-D2 knew that Anakin wouldn't let anything bad happen to him. Anakin tracked his little friend across the galaxy until he found the top secret location where Grievous was hiding.

Grievous and his droid army were no match for Anakin. He easily defeated R2's droid captors. The Jedi then used his powers to find and rescue R2, who was very happy to see his Master.

R2-D2 wondered if C-3PO was okay, but his friend was in big trouble. Much like what General Grievous had done, Cad Bane had captured C-3PO because of the secret information he had about the Republic.

This wouldn't be the first time R2 had to rescue a friend.
Once, he was exploring a wrecked starship on the planet
Vanqor with Anakin and Jedi Master Mace Windu. They
were looking for clues as to why the ship crashed.

But once they got inside the wreckage, the damaged ship collapsed and Anakin and Mace were trapped inside. R2-D2 was their only hope. The little droid had to get back to their ships and send out a rescue message.

But when he got to the ships, a mighty gundark was waiting for him. It was sitting right on top of Anakin's starfighter. R2-D2 was tough, but he was afraid that a gundark might be more than he could handle.

Then he had an idea. R2 used his thruster jets to rocket off
the ship. He knew the gundark would chase after him. True
enough, the gundark leaped into the air—but R2-D2 was
too fast.

Once the gundark was off Anakin's starfighter, R2-D2 blasted a cable that attached to the ship and remotely started the ship's engines. As the ship powered up, the gundark charged at R2. The little droid waited for the monster to get closer.

Just as the gundark was about to pounce, R2 shot the other end of the cable around the gundark. The monster paused for a second before the cable pulled tight. At that moment the gundark realized it was attached to the starfighter.

R2-D2 safely landed on Mace Windu's starfighter and tried to send out a distress signal, but a ship full of bounty hunters blocked the signal. R2 blasted off in the starfighter. He had to find a way to rescue his friends.

On Vanqor, Mace was worried.

"Your droid has been gone for too long," Mace said to Anakin. "He must have failed to deliver your message."

"Artoo will come through," Anakin replied, knowing that he could trust his little friend.

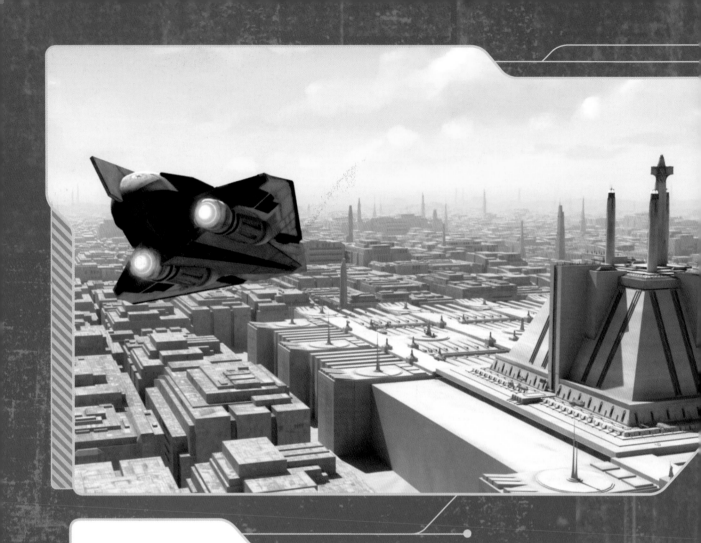

Once he escaped the bounty hunters, R2-D2 flew the starfighter all the way back to the Jedi Temple on Coruscant. The Jedi would know what to do—they'd have a plan to rescue Anakin and Mace.

Jedi Master Plo Koon quickly ordered a team of clone troopers to go to Vanqor. They had to act fast. There was no telling how long Anakin and Mace would survive being trapped in the rubble.

R2-D2 led Plo Koon and the clone troopers to the crash site. He remembered exactly where Anakin and Mace were trapped. The clone troopers piloted the Republic gunship alongside the crash site and the Jedi rescued their friends.

"Come here, droid," Mace called to R2 after he and Anakin had been rescued. "I can see why your master trusts you." R2 knew that C-3PO trusted him, too. He had to move quickly.

R2-D2 learned a lot from Anakin and the other Jedi. He knew that he had to be brave and try to find his friend— even if it was his fault that his friend went missing. If he found C-3PO, he'd never leave his side again.

He asked every droid that he could find if they'd seen his friend. The city was a big place and C-3PO could be anywhere. R2 wouldn't give up, just like his friends never gave up on him when he got into trouble.

Eventually R2-D2 found his way to where Cad Bane was holding C-3PO. It was a scary place, but R2 knew that he had to fight his fear in order to save his friend. That's what Anakin had always done to protect him.

R2-D2 arrived just in time to rescue his friend. He thought that he might never see C-3PO again.

"Oh, Artoo," C-3PO called. He'd never been so happy to see the little droid.

The two droids headed back home and R2-D2 didn't leave his friend's side the whole way back. He'd learned a valuable lesson about traveling in the city. There were a lot of dangerous people out there, and friends needed to stick together.